Guess What! We're Moving

Christine Harder Tangvald
Illustrated by Benton Mahan

Chariot Books
David C. Cook Publishing Co.

Dedicated to all our wonderful family and friends—from Spokane, Ritzville, and Chehalis, Washington, who helped us through a truly traumatic move. God bless you all.

The Tangvalds

Chariot Books is an imprint of David C. Cook Publishing Co.

David C. Cook Publishing Co., Elgin, Illinois 60120
David C. Cook Publishing Co., Weston, Ontario

GUESS WHAT! WE'RE MOVING
© 1988 by Christine Harder Tangvald for text and Benton Mahan for illustrations.

Cover and interior design by Dawn Lauck

First Printing, 1988

Printed in Singapore
93 92 91 90 89   5 4 3 2

Library of Congress Cataloging-in-Publication Data
Tangvald, Christine Harder.
  Guess what—we're moving!

  (Please help me, God)
  Summary: Describes how to prepare for a move and ways of making it easier to pack, say good-bye, and become acquainted with a new neighborhood, school, church, and friends.
    1. Moving, Household—Juvenile literature.
[1. Moving, Household. 2. Christian life] I. Mahan, Ben, ill. II. Title. III. Series: Tangvald, Christine Harder. Please help me, God.
TX307.T36 1988 648'.9 87-34107
ISBN 1-55513-481-5

Did you know we're moving? We are! We're moving to a different home. Isn't that exciting?

And guess what? We're taking all our stuff with us. We're taking my bed and my favorite toys and our furniture and our dishes and our clothes . . . and just about EVERYTHING!

We're moving from our OLD HOME to our NEW HOME.

Does God know I'm moving?

Oh, yes—of course! God knows everything about EVERYTHING.

That's the best thing about God. He always knows where I am. He knows exactly *where* I am moving, and He knows exactly *when* I am moving.

And God goes *with* me everywhere I go. So God will go with me to my *new home*.

I wonder . . . what will my *new friends* be like?

I like my friends here, and they like me. We play ball and jump rope and climb trees . . . and have lots of fun.

But MAYBE some kids live right next door to my new home. And MAYBE they need a friend—like ME—even a *best friend*.

MAYBE my *new* friends will like to play ball and jump rope and climb trees.

MAYBE my new friends will have a tire swing or a bicycle or different toys than I have, and we can SHARE. Yes, I'm *sure* I will like my new friends.

Can I invite my *new* friends to our *new* home for ice-cream cones?

I hope my new friends like to:
1. Go swimming.
2. Play hide-and-seek.
3. _pee_____.
4. _pee and poop._

I wonder . . . what will my *new school* be like?

I really like my old school. My friends are fun, and my teacher is nice.

But MAYBE my new school is close to my home and I can walk. Or MAYBE I will get to ride the bus! MAYBE my new school has a swing *and* a slide!

My new teacher will be very, very nice.

Yes, I'm *sure* I will like my new school.

GOD will help us find a *new church!*

MAYBE our new church will have lots of kids. And MAYBE our new church will be close to my home. And MAYBE our new church will have a pastor who smiles a lot.

We can go to Sunday school and potluck dinners and worship services and Vacation Bible School.

People will like us RIGHT AWAY in our new church.

TAKE-ALONG BAG

I'm packing a TAKE-ALONG BAG, a bag I can take along *with* me when we move.

I'm picking out a few of my favorite things to take right with me. I think I will choose:

1. My jump rope.
2. My favorite little toy.
3. _____ .
4. _____ .
5. _____ .

Here's some other fun stuff I can put in my TAKE-ALONG BAG!

1. Color crayons and color books.
2. A soft, stuffed animal.
3. THIS BOOK!
4. A rubber ball.
5. A small flashlight.
6. _____ .
7. _____ .
8. _____ .

It will be fun to keep my TAKE-ALONG BAG right with me when we move.

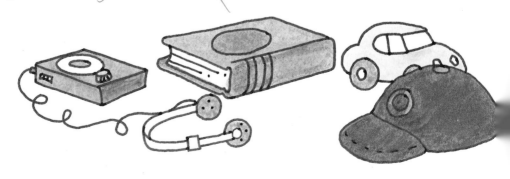

RIGHT-AWAY BOX

My family is packing a RIGHT-AWAY BOX—things we'll want RIGHT AWAY when we get to our new home, like:

1. Our picnic dishes.
2. Pictures of Grandpa and Grandma.
3. Our family Bible.

4. _____ .

5. _____ .

Each person gets to choose things to put into our RIGHT-AWAY BOX. I think I might choose:

1. My favorite pillow.
2. My night-light.

3. _____ .

4. _____ .

These are some of the things I want RIGHT AWAY in my *new home!*

IMPORTANT NAMES AND ADDRESSES TO REMEMBER!

Important old friends:

Name	Address	Phone
1.		
2.		
3.		
4.		

Important new friends:

Name	Address	Phone
1.		
2.		
3.		
4.		

I can still talk to Grandma and Grandpa on the phone. I can write a letter to my *best* friend, and I can send a postcard to my Sunday school class.

AUTOGRAPH PAGE
Old Friends and New Friends

A TREASURE HUNT
IN MY NEW NEIGHBORHOOD
Old Friends and New Friends

PUT AN ☒ IN THE BOX WHEN YOU FIND:

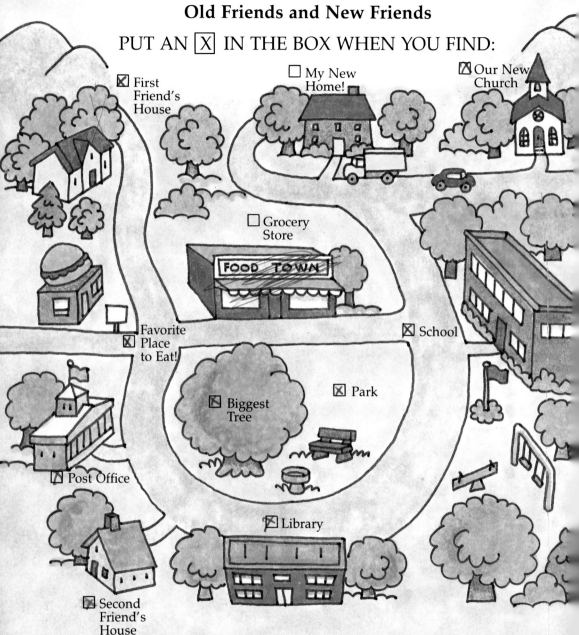

☒ First Friend's House

☐ My New Home!

☒ Our New Church

☐ Grocery Store

FOOD TOWN

☒ Favorite Place to Eat!

☒ School

☒ Biggest Tree

☒ Park

☒ Post Office

☒ Library

☒ Second Friend's House

Today I got to pick something out at our new

grocery store: _____ .

Today I met: _____ .

TEN SUGGESTIONS FOR PARENTS

The decision is *made*.
You *are* moving.
What an adventure for the whole family! Moving can be exciting and fun. It can also be intimidating and scary. Here are some positive suggestions to help bridge the transition from the OLD HOME to the NEW HOME.

1. **Remove the fear of the unknown.**
   As soon as possible, do something to make the new home real and concrete to the child. Before you move, visit the new home with the child if possible. If not, try to get a picture. Send to the Chamber of Commerce for information and brochures about your new community.

   Assure your child the future place has a house, a park, a school, etc. The more you can do to make it a *known* quantity, the better.

2. **Allow—even plan for—a few tears.**
   Do not add *guilt* to *grief* by saying, "Big boys (and girls) don't cry." Big boys (and girls) DO CRY! Let the grief out. Don't dwell on it, but also don't ignore it.

   Allow the children to see *your* emotions. Then they will know it is OK to cry or to be happy and excited.

3. **Include the child in future planning.**
   Replace the feeling of anxiety with a feeling of *anticipation* by adopting a spirit of adventure. Include activities your family will look forward to:

   On the way, we will stop at _____

   Once a day we will _____

   Next month we will _____

4. **Emphasize the positive.**
   Pick one or two positive aspects of the move to emphasize—something tangible and meaningful to the child. For example:
   I will have my own room/bigger room.
   We will camp out along the way.
   We will visit relatives enroute.

5. **Plan for success.**
   Promise only realistic things. Be careful not to build dreams of unreal expectations (for yourself or for the child). Be *honest*. If it is a long trip, say so.

   Also, be sure everyone gets enough *rest*—including you—as well as lots of *hugs* and *kisses*!

6. **Be flexible.**
   Adopt an attitude of flexibility, and allow for a few mistakes. If
   something goes wrong, which it probably will, give each other a *hug*
   and go on from there.

7. **Be enthusiastic.**
   At least part of the time! Attitude is so important, and enthusiasm is
   catching. Even in short spurts, enthusiasm can turn periods of
   transition into quality time. Also allow yourself some time for your
   own emotions.
   Remember: *The best you can do is the best you can do!*

8. **Include the *church* in your move.**
   A new church can become the center of your new community. The
   church is not only a place of worship, but also a place of *fellowship* and
   support and *contacts.*
   *Wherever you go, God has prepared a community of believers to welcome
   and support you in His love!*
   As soon as possible, involve your family in your new church's
   activities—VBS, Sunday school, potluck dinners, etc. Make your new
   church a *focal point* for your family.

9. **Include *God* in your move.**
   Hold hands and pray together—short, informal prayers in your own
   words. Ask for His divine direction and guidance.
   This gives your family the *knowledge* of the *security* and *authority* of
   God. And that is not only good for moving day, but for *any* day!

10. **Use this book . . .**
    as a starting point for ideas and activities. Help your child fill in the
    blanks, or draw pictures if he can't write yet.
    Feel free to elaborate on the suggestions and recommendations. For
    example:
    Expand the Autograph and Picture page into a poster on butcher
    paper.
    Include an outline of each person's hand.
    Pack stamps, envelopes, postcards, and pens in the Take-Along
    Bag to send letters to family and favorite friends.
    Include a copy of *medical* and *school records* in the Right-Away Box.

*May God richly bless your family and help you
bond into a stronger unit as you face this new
challenge . . . together!*

Christine Harder Tangvald